HEY, DIDDLE DIDDLE

KIN EAGLE

ILLUSTRATED BY ROB GILBERT

WHISPERING COYOTE PRESS

DALLAS

An Our House Book

Published by Whispering Coyote Press
300 Crescent Court, Suite 860
Dallas, TX 75201
Text copyright © 1997 by Kin Eagle
Illustrations copyright © 1997 by Rob Gilbert

10 9 8 7 6 5 4 3 2

Book design and production by *The Kids at Our House*
Text was set in 17-point Tiffany Medium
Printed in Italy by STIGE Turin
Library of Congress Cataloging–in–Publication Data

Eagle, Kin, 1964
    Hey diddle, diddle / written by Kin Eagle; illustrated
by Roby Gilbert.
        p.   cm.
    Summary: This nonsense tale continues the story of the
traditional rhyme in which the cow jumps over the moon.
    ISBN 1-879089-007-5
    [1. Cows—Fiction.   2.Stories in rhyme.]
I. Gilbert, Roby, 1963–   ill.   II. Title.
PZ8.3E112515He   1997
[Fic]—dc20   96–12763
                                              CIP
                                              AC

For Sam and Toni,
and for Adam, Jonathan, and Benjamin
—K.E.

For Juliette and Sky,
with all my love
—R.G.

Hey, diddle diddle,
the cat and the fiddle,
the cow jumped over the moon.

The little boy laughed
to see such a sight
and the dish ran away with the spoon.

The puss with the fiddle
asked his new friend a riddle:
"What's black, what's white, and brown, too?"
"Don't know," said the cow,
"I give up, tell me now."
And they laughed, "Silly cow, why it's you!"

The cow was out grazing
when just then—amazing!—
she suddenly leaped to the moon.

But she jumped with such might,
she went past it that night!
I don't think she'll be coming back soon.

The boy, he was feeling
like running and squealing,
"Cows don't belong up in the stars!"
Though it seemed from that spot
that she traveled a lot,
the cow only made it to Mars.

While up there in space,
the cow made a face
because she had wanted to know
what the dish and the spoon,
so far from the moon,
were doing on the planet below.

The dish and the spoon
ran into Baboon,
who had never before in his life

seen a spoon and a dish,
who at least didn't wish,
they were joined by a fork and a knife.

Baboon and the boy
sat and played with a toy,
as the cat danced into the room.

Then the boy and the cat
(who was terribly fat)
did a jig with the mop and the broom.

Hey, Yankee Doodle!
The cat loved the poodle;
you'd think they always would fight.

But they loved each other
like sister and brother
and so it seemed perfectly right.

The boy and the cat
relaxed as they sat
when some dust fell down from the moon.

They looked up from the ground,
saw the cow floating down
and she squealed as she fell on Baboon.

The cow and Baboon,
the dish and the spoon,
the cat and the fiddle and boy,
don't care what they play,
as long as each day
is filled with laughter and joy!